Other Mouse Village titles available:

Welcome to Mouse Village
Jack Mouse and the Scarecrow
Matt Mouse and the Big Surprise
Myrtle Mouse and the Naughty Twins

First published in Great Britain in 2000 by Madcap Books,
André Deutsch Ltd, 76 Dean Street, London, W1V 5HA

www.vci.co.uk

A catalogue record for this book is available from the British Library

Design by Traffika Publishing Ltd
Reprographics by Digicol Link

ISBN 0 233 99574 9

Printed in Belgium by Proost nv

AMANDA MOUSE
AND THE
BIRTHDAY CAKE

by Gyles Brandreth

Illustrated by Mary Hall

MADCAP

Welcome to the Thatched Cottage! Who lives here? Donald Duck? Freddie Frog? Dobbin the Donkey? Don't be silly! This is Mouse Village. Only mice live here, and the mouse who lives in this house is one of the nicest mice you'll ever meet. She's neat, she's sweet, and her name is Amanda.

Amanda Mouse is a happy mouse. And a busy mouse. She loves cooking; she's an excellent cook. Nobody in Mouse Village bakes better gingerbread mice. Amanda also loves painting; she's a fine artist. Nobody in Mouse Village paints prettier pictures than Amanda Mouse.

A manda does have one small problem.
'If I could remember what it was,' she says,
'I'd tell you about it. Oh, good, I've
just remembered. I keep forgetting things. That's
my problem.'

Yes, Amanda Mouse is very forgetful.

'Where have I put my apron? Oh, silly me,
I've got it on!'

So far, today, Amanda hasn't forgotten anything. In fact, she's remembered something rather special. It's her best friend's birthday.

Amanda's best friend is Myrtle Mouse, who runs the Mouse Village Tea Shop, and on Myrtle's birthday Amanda always remembers to bake Myrtle a beautiful birthday cake.

Amanda takes her wooden spoon and mixes the eggs and the flour and the sugar and the cocoa powder. She pours the cake mixture into her baking tin and pops it into her piping-hot oven. It smells so good, and it's going to taste delicious!

'Now, Amanda Mouse,' she says to herself, 'What have you forgotten? I know! Candles! You can't have a birthday cake without candles.'

So Amanda puts on her hat and her coat and her little white gloves. She picks up her purse and her shopping basket and off she trots, along the lane, past Flora's Flower Stall and into the High Street. Outside the Sweet Shop she says hello to Mrs Sugar.

'Where are you off to?' asks Mrs Sugar.

'Oh dear,' says Amanda, 'I can't remember.'

'You'll forget your own birthday next,' laughs Mrs Sugar.

'That's it!' shouts Amanda, 'Candles for the birthday cake!'

Amanda Mouse hurries across the High Street and into the Corner Shop. 'What can I get for you today?' asks Charlie Mouse.

'Candles, please,' says Amanda Mouse.

'Candles, eh? Are you baking a birthday cake?' asks Charlie.

'Yes,' says Amanda.

'How lovely!' says Charlie.

'Oh dear,' squeals Amanda, 'I've just remembered – I've left the cake in the oven. I'd better go home.' And off she scampers, as fast as her dainty feet will carry her.

When Amanda gets to her front door, she remembers that she's forgotten her key! Poor Amanda Mouse, locked out of her own house. She pushes open the letter box. She can smell the cake baking in the oven. She calls through the letter box, 'Is anybody there?'

'Locked out?' asks Matt Mouse, the Mouse Village postmouse.

'Oh,' squeaks Amanda, turning round. 'It's you, Matt. You gave me quite a surprise.'

'Don't worry,' says Matt, jumping onto his bicycle, 'I'll sort you out.' And off he goes.

When Matt Mouse returns, he has the Mouse Village Fire Brigade with him! 'Oh dear,' squeaks Amanda, 'What a lot of trouble I've caused.'

'Not to worry,' says Fergus the Fire Chief. 'We're here to help.'

The fire brigade sets to work, putting up the long ladder for Fergus to climb. Fergus then makes his way onto the beautiful thatched roof of the cottage.

'I'm going down the chimney,' he says, and disappears.

W hat happens next? You've guessed: all
is well. Fergus opens the front door
from the inside and the cake is saved,
just in time.

'Thank you,' says Amanda Mouse, 'And now you've
saved the cake, you must all have some.' Amanda gives
a slice of cake to each member of the fire brigade. And
she gives a special piece to Matt.

'That's the best chocolate cake I've ever tasted,' says
Fergus the Fire Chief, licking his lips.

Just as they finish the last crumb of cake, somebody knocks on the door. Can you guess who? Of course. It's Myrtle Mouse.

'Oh dear,' squeals Amanda, 'I'd forgotten you were coming!'

'Don't worry,' says Myrtle with a laugh. 'I knew you would.'

'And we've eaten all your birthday cake!'

'Don't worry, I've brought another cake from the Tea Shop, and Charlie Mouse has given me the candles you forgot.'

'The one thing I haven't forgotten is your present, Myrtle,' says Amanda proudly. 'I'm going to give you a picture for your birthday, and I'm going to paint it now!'

And when they've sung 'Happy Birthday' and had another slice of cake, Amanda gets out her paints and her paintbrushes and paints a really lovely picture of them all.

'I won't forget this birthday,' says Myrtle Mouse, delighted with her picture.

Will you?